Don't Feed The Bully

Brad Tassell

Llessat Publishing
Santa Claus, IN

Don't Feed The Bully

Copyright © 2006 by Brad Tassell
Illustration Copyright © 2006 by Brad Tassell and Logan Sibrel

Llessat Publishing
Box 742
Santa Claus, IN 47579

Library of Congress Control Number:
2006908187

International Standard Book Number:
ISBN-10: 0-89708-235-4
ISBN-13: 978-0-89708-235-8
  2 3 4 5 6 7 8 9 10

School & library purchases, wholesale inquiries:
The Distributors
702 S. Michigan
South Bend, IN 46601
orders@thedistributors.com
Toll Free Ordering: 800-348-5200

For Janet and Darby

I am Hannibal Greatneck III, and I am a detective. My job is to watch, to observe human nature, and see things no one else sees, finding hidden clues until the pattern of evidence points to one conclusion. Thus, unraveling the mystery and solving what no one could solve.

1

My greatest case started as no case at all. The case I call "Don't Feed the Bully" started on my first day as a transfer student at William B. Travis elementary school. Bells should have rung in my head immediately, but it wasn't until weeks later I realized the connection. Colonel William B. Travis was the commander of the Alamo in 1836 where he and 187 other men fought off Santa Anna and 2,999 other bullies for ten days before being over run like a golf cart in a demolition derby.

I should have figured it. Any school with such a name-sake could have a warped sense of dealing with bullies and make sure to stop any present day Santa Annas from over-running them.

Ending my elementary school career at William Travis in Mrs. Austin's sixth grade class was not my plan. Dad was changing jobs, and I needed to follow my meal ticket as eleven-year-old detectives don't rake in the kind of dough needed to satisfy a root beer and Cheeto habit that kept my dentist on his toes and my fingertips consistently pale orange.

It didn't take a master sleuth to spot the first major difference in Mrs. Austin's classroom from any other in my previous elementary career. I am not talking about the pair of hard hazel eyes, tight curly red hair, pasty white skin, and serious prepubescent acne standing directly in front of me like a pint-size border guard as I walked through the door.

"I am Kurt Pesterman," he said in a tone that stunk of superiority, as if judging people was Kurt's hobby and I was a new project. "I welcome you to William Travis Elementary," the welcome was as empty as a free milk bowl in Cat Town.

"I am president of the WBT Agitator Awareness Society, and you are?"

I figured, being new, I shouldn't make waves in the first thirty seconds in a classroom I'd be spending the next 132 weekdays with time off for Christmas, spring break, and a possible two-day stomach flu I was planning for late January during the 48-hour Sam Spade marathon on the Sleuth Channel. I calmly gave my name, "Hannibal Greatneck III, friends call me Handy."

"Well, Mr. Greatneck," he said as if only what he said was important and being friends was a condition of me knowing that importance. "You aren't big enough to be a physical threat, so I will just let you know we also don't tolerate verbal bullying either."

Kurt smiled a row of pickled yellow teeth that seemed to flinch when exposed as if they rarely saw the light.

"There are severe penalties for breaking the code of respectful conduct in this class, and the school."

All of this explained the observation which I had not finished before I was confronted by WBT's agitator welcoming committee.

A CAGE!

An actual cage was sitting in the middle of the classroom. A desk sat in the center, and all the other desks were around the outside mocking the virus that they found a way to tolerate.

"That is where Ralphie sits," Kurt said as if the Agitator Awareness Society was also dabbling in mind reading.

"Ralphie, a chimpanzee?"

"More like a Gorilla," Kurt Pesterman said in a smirking tone as if he'd made a joke, but laughing was beneath him. "Ralphie has strong bullying tendencies."

"Tendencies?" I asked.

"Pushing kids down, intimidating smaller kids, he used to take food from other kids' trays in the lunch room. That's why the sign."

I looked up at the cage and couldn't believe it had escaped me before. In bold purple letters across a bright pink sign over the front of the cage were the words, "Don't Feed the Bully."

"That sign reminds Ralphie what he's not supposed to do. As I said, penalties." Kurt I could see was very proud of himself and added, "I call it literal motivation."

Ralphie lumbered in as if he had been waiting in the hall for someone to say penalties before he could enter. He was huge for twelve and he grumbled to himself as he pushed chairs out of the way. The other students who had been filing in during Pesterman's and my chat froze, possum caught in the bat signal. A wave of fear swept the room as Ralphie heaved his massive hulking person inside the cage and shut the door with a slam that echoed penitentiary off every wall. Within seconds, things went back to normal. It could have been because I was new, but the fear from the class registered 15 out of 10 on the over-reaction scale. It looked like they all were trained to flinch at Ralphie's every move. Ralphie was big, but I'd seen a lot meaner, and yet nobody had ever shown the kind of terror I'd seen in the eyes of my new classmates. Was Ralphie what they were afraid of or did his presence remind them of something else?

"Isn't this a little severe for fingering a few tater tots," I spit out as I realized I'd put my foot so far into my mouth I could have performed a tonsillectomy with my Nike swoosh.

Kurt Pesterman's mood turned in an instant from grandma to the big bad wolf, and I was Little Red. His eyes and manner became severe, "Well, maybe Mr. Greatneck III, if you had been the butt of the bully's wrath. Had you suffered innumerable cosmic wedgies? Had you tasted the degradation of a swirly? Had you stood by in horror as Mr. Crumblebean was torn apart before your eyes to a symphony of laughter, and seen the devastation that it can wreak. You would not be as flippant with your diagnosis."

Kurt's veins began to burn a brilliant blue right through the skin of his neck and forehead like a 3-D road map. His face began to battle his hair for the reddest thing on his head. I could tell Kurt had spent some time being bullied, probably mercilessly, and now that he held the upper hand, he was not conceding an inch. I just wondered if maybe he was enjoying this power a little too much.

"Sorry, man," I said, looking around the room at 23 faces that were staring at me with the same kind of fear and trepidation reserved for Scooby Doo and Shaggy the first time the swamp monster shows up near the Mystery Machine. I suddenly wasn't sure who they feared more, Ralphie or Kurt. I snapped back with my most sheepish "awe shucks" humble pie voice, "It's my first day and I don't know what's happening. I just want to make friends. I guess since I read a lot of Encyclopedia Brown books, I ask a lot of questions that don't need answers."

The color or more precisely, the lack of color, returned to Kurt's face as the redness of his temper faded like a stress bruise. His veins sunk slowly back below skin level, little submarines waiting for their next trip to the surface.

Kurt spoke in a tense but guarded tone, "Since it is your first day Mr. Greatneck, I will let that little slip go as a sign of ignorance, but watch yourself as we do not treat agitators lightly." That part was as clear as simple addition to a college senior, but I was a little sketchy on the criteria the "we" used to separate the agitators from the detectives.

As Mrs. Austin entered the room, the class took their seats and Kurt went over to greet our teacher like a terrier that hadn't seen its owner in months and might wet the rug with excitement.

Things settled down to a pop quiz that would not count for me. I began to try and wrap my brain around the new school, new situations, and new people. Why was everybody so scared of Ralphie? Why was everyone even more scared of Kurt? How did someone get a huge cage into a classroom? Why did the teacher seem to have no problem with any of this? Who was Mr. Crumblebean? There was a mystery here, and I probably should have finished the day and begged my mom for home schooling until 7th grade. But I can't help myself. Help was needed. People were scared, and I have to get to the truth.

2

If I were going to jump headlong into the rattler's den, I did not want to start with the biggest snake. So, I would stay out of Kurt's way as much as possible until all roads led to his door. The problem was: a guy that small who instills that much fear must have more eyes than a banana crate full of tarantulas. I needed to take Kurt's advice and watch my step, watch the questions I asked, and watch to whom I asked them. I figured Mrs. Austin was the best first target. If she thought I were being too meddlesome,

I could just make as if I were sugar crazy from extra Twinkies.

I waited until the entire class had left for recess and Ralphie was let go with a warning from Kurt to keep to himself on the playground. Ralphie shrugged and plodded out the door. Kurt started to hang back, but must have decided that the new kid might need to talk to the teacher on his first day of school, and there was little threat to him if I spoke to Mrs. Austin alone. He left with the flare of a matador as he flipped his coat around his back.

***

"Hannibal Greatneck III, it is nice to have you in my class," Mrs. Austin said, sunny as fresh orange juice.

"My friends call me Handy."

"Okay Handy, I am sure we will be friends. I hope you will have a splendid year here. I have put a packet together to get you up to speed since the semester is already one third over. Although, your record from your previous school says you are a very smart boy and your grades are excellent. You also got a 98% on my pop quiz. So, it seems you are already up to speed."

"Thank you, Mrs. Austin. I try to keep up as best I can," I said. I can't say I do not enjoy a compliment, but humility gets you a lot farther than cockiness, and I still needed information.

"Do you have any questions for me?" asked Mrs. Austin, saving me from asking if I could ask any questions.

"Yes ma'am, I do," I said. "Isn't it odd to have a cage in the middle of the classroom?"

Mrs. Austin smiled as if I asked about the feeding habits of the class hamster.

"Oh, that," Mrs. Austin said as if she just noticed the cage herself. "We here at Travis used to have a terrible bullying problem. The teachers, the parents, the PTA, and the principal were all beside themselves with worry about how to help. Kurt, alone, was a nervous wreck, others were scared stiff, and grades were suffering. The teachers never saw anything first hand which makes it doubly hard to make corrections. We were having tons of complaints, and not just about Ralphie. He is actually a nice boy, but just sometimes, I guess he can't control himself around smaller kids."

"Like Kurt," I said, getting a good picture.

"Like Kurt," she said. "So, after the Mr. Crumblebean incident something had to be done. We brought in parents, had meetings, but no one could get a handle on all the complaints. One day we decided to ask the kids to try to come up with a solution. They came up with the WBT Agitators Society with certain rules and punishments for bullying."

"Mrs. Austin?" I interrupted. "Who came to you with the kid's solution?"

"Oh, hmm," she said, looking up and right, which psychologists will tell you is what people do when accessing their memory or lying. I did not think Mrs. Austin was lying.

"I think it was Kurt. Yes, he created the society concept, filled its membership, and they created the rules and punishments, or rather corrections. This, as you will see, has stopped bullying almost totally."

"What about the cage?" I asked, thinking it resembled an alien science experiment rather than an elementary school.

"That was actually Ralphie's idea," she said, still a little surprised by the sound of it herself. My brain skipped a cog. Did Mrs. Austin just tell me that Ralphie had asked to spend his last year of elementary school locked up like a half-trained bear?

"Ralphie walked in one day and said he wanted to sit in a cage?" I asked, trying to drain the skepticism from my voice.

"No, Ralphie was getting in trouble three times a week. Kurt mentioned it as an obvious deterrent, and Ralphie decided it might help him control himself. The society voted. It seems to have worked. While Ralphie has been in there, all bullying complaints through the society have stopped."

"Through the society?" I asked, alarms going off in my head like a fire at an orphanage. "Do all bullying problems go through the society first?"

"Yes. All complaints first go through the society. After penalties are assessed, the complaints are given to me, and I haven't gotten one this year."

I was getting an idea of what was going on, but needed a lot more information and actual evidence. The faculty was being made happy by having the wool pulled so far over their eyes that all they could smell was six feet of sheep. I had to start talking to anyone who would talk. Things were so bad that Ralphie would sit in a cage to get some peace. Did he know he was being used, not just as an example to any other potential bully, but to any critic of the Agitator Awareness Society? Conform or your life will be destroyed.

Could I get Ralphie to talk to me? Who was in the WBT Agitator Awareness Society? Why did everybody fear Kurt Pesterman? Should I? Who was Mr. Crumblebean? It wasn't even lunch and I was hip deep in a quagmire that Magellan couldn't navigate.

3

I headed out to the playground to sniff around for clues. William B. Travis's playground looked like any other. Kids mostly played with their own age groups, then splintered off like the cast of *The Lion King*. The Monkey kids were climbing and swinging in endless loops. The Okapi kids or chasers ran after each other in perpetual circles. The grazers were standing in packs like groups of Zebras gossiping. The players, who like any Serengeti cubs, played non-stop games – kickball, tetherball, or any sports that satisfied their boundless energy stream and need for competition like head-butting rams.

There were also the Meerkats – the kids who scrambled nervously on the playground from end to end just trying to keep out of everyone's way, and trying to eke out an existence as the lowest arc on the circle of life. One big difference between William B. Travis and the rest of the world's elementary playgrounds was the king of beasts had been defeated, dethroned, and didn't seem to care. Ralphie sat alone on a step. On the top of Pride Rock was Kurt Pesterman.

Here *The Lion King* reference ends because Kurt was no Scar. He was a Meerkat, but a Meerkat who figured a way to crush the societal evolution and mold his own reality. He didn't even have any Hyenas for help. The other bigger sixth grade boys, who outside this "Bizarro World" would have lorded over the domain, with Ralphie as king, had shrunken away and avoided him like he was wearing skunk perfume. Yet, they were not aligning themselves with Kurt either. Kurt ruled alone and needed no army to hold power. Even the other Meerkats steered clear of him. Kurt was a hard guy to like. I would have thought the labeled geeks, nerds, and dorks would have crawled out of the woodwork for a chance to taste the power a predator-free landscape had to offer. I was more puzzled than my mom with an X-box.

From behind me, I heard a small high-pitched throat clearing – softly, as if only partly sure it wanted attention. I turned around and ran into a smile so cute that my optic nerves had to squeeze tight to hold my eyeballs in my head. The only thing that kept me conscious was that men in my family are late bloomers, and the hormones that make adolescent boys slobbering boneheads around girls were at least four years away.

"Hewow," I stammered, hoping she heard more of the hello and less of the wow.

"Hi," she said, in a voice that could make a choir of angels give up and become mimes. "I'm, uh…Kayla."

The fact that she was as nervous as I was brought my strength back to normal, but I could still feel the gnawing of puppy love grinding away my common sense.

"Handy?" I replied with a small squeak that made it sound like a question.

"At what?" Kayla said confused, as I mentally slapped my palm onto my forehead. I cleared my throat.

"No, I mean Handy is what people call me. It's short for Hannibal." That was better.

"Oh, hello Handy," she said, looking as if she should maybe quickly invent a time machine and go back in time about 45 seconds.

"Don't worry," I said. "I am a whiz at second impressions." Kayla relaxed a little bit.

"You made a good impression when you walked into class this morning." She continued, "You handled yourself very well with Kurt."

"Thanks," I said and dove off the high dive. "Why is everyone so afraid of Kurt?" Kayla's eyes drooped, and I could see I had moved too fast, destroying any chance of real answers. Kayla recovered her composure quickly and smiled another cutie pie smile, albeit a more melancholy one.

"You seem like a nice and smart kid, Handy," she said, "like my little brother."

Little brother I thought. Ouch! That spelled doom for even an eleven-year-old's version of romance. "I'd keep playing the humble new kid and just do your homework," Kayla said, and she began to turn away.

"Kayla," I said, wondering what she meant by homework. "You came up to me for a reason. Maybe I can help."

Kayla turned back. "I don't need help," Kayla responded, with a knowing squint in her eyes that signaled many people did need help.

"I can see that."

"I just wanted to say welcome to William B. Travis,"

she said, as she floated away, a pixie from Neverland, and me out of dust and low on good thoughts.

***

The bell rang with an anemic thud and we all ambled, ran, or plodded back to class. A creepy feeling crawled up my spine as my peripheral vision caught a glimpse of burning hazel. Kurt was eyeballing me harder than a crazed fan at the Oscars from across the four square court. I pretended not to notice and walked in with some of the kickball crowd to see about playing a little short stop. Kurt was smart, and I think dangerous. His look meant I had better watch my step.

4

A few days went by with little headway and the same avoidance of what was standing in the classrooms and halls of William B. Travis like a 2,000-pound rhino that no one wanted to notice. Ralphie stayed in his cage, I played some kickball, and no one would talk. The underlying tension that gripped every student was as apparent as it was ignored. It reminded me of when my five-year-old cousin Lucy comes to my house. She follows me around asking a million dumb questions, and I pretend she is not giving her dolls rides down the stairs on my skateboard.

I asked my classmates questions and got little feedback. People seemed to like me, but whenever I asked about the Society, the cage, Kurt, or Ralphie they would clam up tighter than a three-year-old mouth at a brussel sprout convention.

I needed to talk to Ralphie and get him into my confidence. The hard part was the approach. I figured the playground was the best place. Ralphie always sat alone on the concrete wall next to the school stairs across and right of the kickball diamond. I needed a plan that would get me close to Ralphie. I went home after the last bell and told Mom that I needed to think. I skipped dinner and took a six-pack of root beer and two bags of Cheetos into my room. This was going to take a lot of thought.

During the next morning recess, I put the plan into motion. My first move was to ask to play catcher for the ritual pre-lunch kickball game.

"Catcher" in kickball is what they call a "loose" term, meaning it had less to do with catching than a half pipe had to do with plumbing. A position reserved for kids with sprained ankles, and kids who could not catch a ball even if it was tattooed to their chest.

No one struck out in kickball so the catcher spent his time retrieving foul kicks and staying out of the way when a team-mate hurled the ball at a runner heading to home plate. A small net could play catcher and plenty of times you didn't even have that, but today I needed to be the net.

Usually being picked within the first three rounds of any game, it was going to look suspicious if I said I wanted to be catcher. I had to use a ruse.

My ruse was a twisted knee that I told everybody I had incurred while jumping from the top bunk of my bed to the Nerf hoop for an atomic 360 double-pump slam dunk. The group nodded their heads with a "been there" smirk and my position was fixed.

***

As catcher, I had to bide my time until Crazy Foot Foreman came to the plate. Chase Foreman could catch any ball that came within a three-state region of his hands, but he couldn't kick to save his life, or the lives of his family, friends, and assorted neighborhood pets. That is why we called him Crazy Foot. He couldn't throw either. The best thing to do, if you were running bases and Crazy Foot had a bead on you with the ball for a leg-stinging out, was to simply stand still. Stop running at all costs. Moving meant fate might lend a hand and you'd be hit by the seventeenth ricochet off the social studies teacher's car. Stand still and Chase, without fail, would throw the ball into the cafeteria kitchen.

Today I needed the foot. Chase couldn't coordinate his foot in front of the ball. He would make a million little corrections in angle and slant of his foot and leg as he swung his lower extremity toward the rolling ball. It looked like someone swinging a wet ferret with a one-pound dumbbell tied to the end. The ball would fly in directions that confused God and could make Isaac Newton throw out his laws of motion and only eat applesauce.

***

It was a long night of planning, but after five root beers, three quarters of a bag of Cheetos, and a bathroom door connected to my room, I had my bases covered.

I needed just a little luck to get Crazy Foot to kick the ball to the extreme right and slightly backwards toward Ralphie. My real lucky charm is that I leave little to chance. Easy part finished. I was catcher and Crazy Foot was coming to kick. He'd have to have an outside pitch and hit the ball with the outside of his foot. It doesn't take eighth-grade algebra to know a rolling object hitting the outside of another object coming toward it on the outside will deflect away and possibly back. At least I think it meant that.

Suddenly, I also thought that this was actually physics, not algebra, and we didn't take that for another four years. No matter, the plan was still good and to make it better I needed reverse psychology, a subject that would not appear until college. Every parent starts playing the reverse psychology card early and often. By age seven, we are immune from its guilt and ramifications.

It was a good bet it would work on Chase, though, because he was a thinker. He mumbled to himself before every kick and his brain talked his body out of doing what it already knew was best. Foreman was a great catcher because he had no time to think. The ball was kicked and he automatically ran to it and it was in his hands, as natural as eating a Snack Pack. A ball rolling toward him, especially nice and slow, gave Chase lots of time to think.

He would psych himself out with every step in the ball's direction until his foot couldn't keep up with the hundreds of contradictory instructions his cerebral cortex was bombarding his muscles with like a single cashier at the day-after-Thanksgiving sale. The result was usually goofy dancing, a quick out, and a small bruise on some kid's head that thought standing behind a wall, facing the street, and in a doorway was a safe distance.

As Chase came to the plate, I only needed a few suggestions to place the odds in my favor.

"Chase, look, left field has more holes than Swiss cheese," I said. A very lame comparison, but I said it in the same voice tone coaches use when they think they are motivating a twelve year-old to greatness.

"You gotta kick it left, man. It's a guaranteed home run."

Chase didn't answer because his mind was already racing toward the speed of light, which incidentally is 186,000 miles per second. I looked it up.

I was half way there. Now I needed a little negative reinforcement.

"Kick right, Chase, and it's an out. They have Callahan in right and next to you; he's the best catcher in the school. Oh, man, and Margaret Hampstead is at second. You know she throws like a bazooka. Kick the ball right and she'll have you for lunch. Not to mention giving you a welt the size of a first grader's head on your back."

Chase began to sweat as I saw a bead of perspiration roll down his temple like a plinko chip. Crazy Foot was thinking a blue streak. One more cog and this machine would start churning out widgets. I threw a little wave at the pitcher. Landon Cruise, who would benefit from an extra slice of pizza during lunch, raised his eyes slowly and squinted. I pointed to the right. The simplest of communications, but it was more effective than GPS. Landon gave me a little shrug, a small nod, and then rolled a perfect pitch just to the right of Crazy Foot. Nice and slow. By this time, Chase's brain had him frantic as his eyes darted from the ball to Margaret to left field. His whole body twitched like a marionette tied to a paint shaker. A newcomer to the scene would have thought Chase was having intense muscle spasms and called 911. We all knew Crazy Foot was simply letting his head play for him as he stumbled and jerked toward the rolling ball.

5

"Little help!"

Ralphie looked at me, down at the ball, pointed at the ball sitting between his feet, and looked away again.

"Well, I did say a 'little' help," I said perplexed at what could have been a confrontational move, but looked more like a stab at humor. I went with my instincts and decided it was an attempt to be funny. "And that was as little help as possible."

Picking up the ball, my brain raced as to what to say next, but Ralphie let me off the hook and surprised me again by speaking. In the few weeks I had been around,

Ralphie had answered a few questions in class, but I could not recall a whole sentence coming out of the cage. His words to me crushed all my biases.

"Glad I could be here for you," Ralphie said, flat and monotone with a slightly perceptible smirk. If a basset hound could talk, he would sound like Ralphie. I was starting to feel stupid that I spent the whole evening planning my ruse to get a chance to talk to Ralphie, and I could have just walked up and said, "Hey."

The words came out slow, but not frustratingly slow, like my first piano teacher who seemed to count to three between syllables. The tempo of Ralphie's speech was even and varied little in pitch. I notice these things because it's easy to tell a bad liar because their voice goes up and down with every fabrication. Ralphie would be a good liar because he only used one note for every sound. If he could sing, he'd have the vocal range of a homing beacon, but low and easy going. I liked it and suddenly liked Ralphie. I again felt like a fool. I was unconsciously avoiding Ralphie too.

I threw the ball back to the game and waved the universal sign for, "You guys go on without me." They went back to the game, and I turned back to Ralphie.

"So, next time I'm drowning, I hope you're there to point out a life preserver," I said.

"Nah, I'd throw you a copy of *Swimming for Dummies*," Ralphie drawled out slow and sarcastic like honey on a Sour Patch Kid. I let his joke hang in the air for what amounted to 17 years.

"Ralphie, what's wrong with this school?" I blurted like a rookie. I was supposed to be the cool one, but Ralphie's utter calm put me off my guard like a lap dog. The rules for getting information from Ellery Queen to Harriet the Spy forbade being whiny. Uncomfortable silence and created confusion was my tool, and I had fallen into my own trap.

One side of Ralphie's mouth lifted a fraction of an inch and I took it for a smile.

"Handy, I am getting good grades for the first time since third grade by minding my own business, not letting my guard down, and keeping to myself. My parents don't automatically get mad when the phone rings because this year it's not about me. They came to school only once and that was open house. That is what's going on at this school."

"But you sit in a cage."

"Didn't you hear, I'm the bully," Ralphie said. "And look around; there are worse positions to be in."

"I don't think you are the bully," I responded. "I think you're giving up your freedom for peace and are scared like the rest of these kids."

Ralphie stood up and was huge. His face hardened like a transformer morphing to action mode. At his full height I was half his size and feeling smaller by the minute. I had to push hard to stop fear from bubbling out of my nostrils. Here was the Ralphie from the cage, and he was scary.

"Well, maybe I didn't mean scared," I said quickly, but words are like Gremlins, you don't recapture them. You never let them out in the first place.

"You don't know what I've done, or how scary I can be!"

I did now. Ralphie wasn't even really raising his voice. He just hardened it like cold steel. The effect was worse than being yelled at by the principal. I stood my ground keeping panic in check. As quickly as he blew up, Ralphie deflated like a touchy puffer fish and sat down. It was a show to illustrate that I should not take Ralphie or his past lightly, and he was not an innocent bystander in the problems at William B. Travis. Ralphie's voice was again lemonade on a back porch.

"Watch yourself Handy. A black eye heels in a week and the girls think you're cool for a while. Other punishments last a lot longer."

Ralphie's statement could have been a threat, but it wasn't. It was advice and friendly advice at that. Ralphie knew from experience that victims often get sympathy, but when they can make you a villain, nobody comes to help you.

I still hadn't found any real answers like who Mr. Crumblebean was, but I was learning lessons that should have been obvious:

1. Do not judge a book by its cover.
2. There are two sides to every story and most people.
3. Being scared stinks!

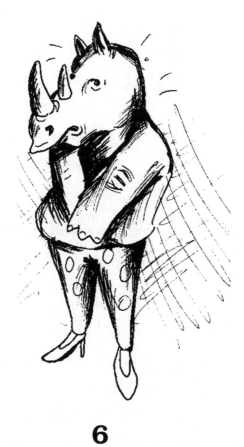

6

If I had thought my fearful moments were done for the day, I was as wrong as stretch pants on a rhino. Heading back to Mrs. Austin's classroom after gym, I noticed my notebook with my homework was not in my book bag. I had just been working on my math at lunch and took my bag with me to gym as usual to save going upstairs to put it in my desk.

It didn't take a master gumshoe to realize I had left the notebook in the locker room because that is the only place my bag had been between lunch and class. Problem was, I never took the notebook out of the bag. I began to smell a setup, and it stunk worse than my gym shorts after a two-mile run.

Someone knew I needed to turn in my homework next period or risk a zero. They also wanted me in the locker room. I was not one to disappoint such a well-planned invitation. I felt somewhat important that someone would go to this much trouble on my behalf. I must be getting close to something. I also was getting a knot in my stomach.

I told Mrs. Austin that I left my notebook in the locker room and may I go get it. She was her regular amiable and oblivious self, but asked me to hurry. Writing a pass, she put down the locker room, the time, and signed her name. The hall pass was a golden ticket of freedom, and it was funny how this little bit of second-hand power gave students a jolt of excitement.

I did a quick-scan attendance count before I walked out of the room. Everybody was in place – Kurt at his desk, Ralphie locked away, and Kayla still cute enough in her chair to cause freshman to try to flunk three times. It looked like I was going to meet some new friends.

***

They came out of the shower as I picked my notebook off the bench in the middle of the room, nowhere near my usual spot, subtle as a sledgehammer to a thumbtack.

"Forget something?" cackled Number One.

A cackle that was immediately recognizable to anyone who has ever been in a school or watched an after-school special, a mix of degrading mockery and threatening humor, and there is always more than one.

"Yeah, looks like Goofyneck is forgetful," Number Two chimed in. I didn't know these two any more than their faces on the playground or in the hall, but someone wanted them to know me. Every sign told me they were about as bright as a flashlight after three years in a junk drawer. They had not come up with this plan themselves. They were enjoying it though. My job now was to stop their enjoyment without escalating them to violence.

They were from the other sixth grade class and one was half a head taller and only using half of his brain, and the other was more than a head taller and borrowing at least a third of the first one's brain. I didn't know their names but if Crabbe and Goyle were to quit Hogwarts, these two could find spots in Slytherin.

They moved into the classic intimidation positions on either side and in front of me. My back was to the row of lockers. Bully radar has tracked on me before, and I keep a few tricks up my sleeve and some cards in my hand, at least until I bluff my way out of this situation:

1. Stay calm.

2. Assess the likelihood of violence.

3. Have a thick skin and a sense of humor.

4. Collect evidence.

(Turn to the first appendix to read each of these steps spelled out in detail.)

***

"Goofyneck, that's funny," I replied. "I can see you guys have done this act before." They were momentarily confused by my comeback and lack of emotion.

"Yeah, well," said Number One, who was a big enough jerk to be up to the challenge of pushing around someone half his size, but his brain lacked the capacity to send the right words to his mouth without instructions from somebody else. He was a 56K modem in a cable modem world. My response had thrown them off the script and these two were not quick enough for improvisation.

"We got a message for you, Sissy Boy," Number Two chimed in, getting the festivities back on track.

"Sissy Boy?" I said. "Is that the message? That I'm a Sissy Boy?"

"Yeah, what are you gonna do, Sissy Boy?" Number One threw in, feeling a little left out and needing to get his bully points in for the judges.

"About what?" I asked.

"No," said Number Two who clearly was working with 2/3 of their collective brain. "The message is: If you want to get along stop doing what you're doing."

"I thought bullying was strictly forbidden at William B. Travis? What if I report you two to the Agitator Awareness Society?" I asked changing the subject. Their laughter brought back the stab of fear that had waned since I began to take control of the situation. These boys had no fear of the Society or its corrections. Did the Society have no real power in stopping bullies, or were they from the Society?

They laughed like Hyenas another half minute leaving me to wonder if they actually needed me here to witness this performance. I suddenly noticed a clue the size of a treasure chest. Hanging halfway out of Number Two's pocket was a hall pass. I needed that little bit of evidence and its information. It had his name, time, and who authorized this little jaunt. The hall pass also said where they were supposed to be going. I was already kicking myself for leaving my digital pen recorder at Grandma's house when I went over there to download old Sam Spade radio shows. Bullies turn on each other in a second when they hear their attacks played back in their own voices. I needed to do something stupid, and against any anti-bullying rule on the books.

"Been nice seeing you girls," I said, as I moved in

toward my new pals as if I was going to leave. Number One was thrilled with his chance to be a bigger part of this project and pushed me up against the lockers. I bounced off the locker, which was a lot louder than it hurt. Number Two picked up the dialogue, "You want to act tough, Goofyneck?"

"Yeah, we're not girls, Goofyneck," said Two. "You're a girl!"

Great comeback genius, I thought as I pretended the slam against the locker hurt more than it did.

"You go when we say," Two sniffed, "and do what we say Sissy Boy."

"Sissy Boy" again – was this guy twelve or six? I could think of about 3,000 crueler and more disgusting things to call someone. I bet their parents never even let them near a PG 13 movie.

I made my final stupid move by stepping over the bench at Number Two, who grabbed me. I kept my arms at my sides and Number Two bear-hugged me awkwardly for a second while, I pulled the slip from his pocket. Two pushed me away, stuck his knuckle out of his fist, and punched it into my arm. That was going to leave a bruise. I showed no pain this time though as a reaction was just what they wanted. I said nothing.

"Is that all you got, Goofyneck? You wanna see who's

a girl?" Number Two made another knuckle-punch fist while Number One looked confused that he was being left out of the punching. Then fate stepped in and the janitor clanked loudly down the steps. We heard him long before we saw him, so there was no chance of any witness, but it did send my errand boys out of my life for the moment.

"What are you doing down here?" the janitor said more as if we were in his way then he cared that we might be in the wrong place.

"We're helping Greatneck get his notebook," said Two.

He looked at me and I stopped rubbing my arm. "Couldn't have found it without them," I said.

The janitor had an inkling of what must be going on, but was not planning on getting involved past a sympathetic look in my direction. I just hoped he wouldn't ask for our hall passes because then Number Two would realize his was gone. The janitor pulled a key chain full of keys enhanced with a large Troll head doll and waved it in our direction.

"You've got your book. Now you three get back to class," the janitor said, before selecting a key to unlock the boiler room. My buddies were up the stairs and gone, and the janitor disappeared into the secret janitor world.

"That went well," I said to myself as I wandered back to class pondering what I now knew and reading Number Two's hall pass:

Name: **Zack Brewer**

Time: **11:35**

Destination: **Counselor's office**

Signed: **Kurt Pesterman**

How did Kurt Pesterman have the power to give hall passes?

I got back to class, handed in my homework, and said it took me so long because someone was punking me and had kicked my notebook under the lockers. Finding it was hard, I had said. Retrieving it was near impossible. I winced when I handed my paper to Mrs. Austin compliments of my new bruise.

"What's wrong?" she asked.

My spider sense was telling me that Kurt Pesterman was paying close attention right now. I could have pulled out the hall pass and told the whole story. Having the hall pass would help prove my story and could get Kurt and my buds in a bit of a sticky position, but chances were slim it would open up the whole vampire's den to the light.

"Hit my arm on the bench when I reached down to get my notebook."

"Okay, honey. Take your seat."

Mrs. Austin was smart, kind, caring, and sensitive, but was so out of touch to being a pre-teen and its problems that if we exploded, she wouldn't even know it for four or five days.

I sat down, noticed Pesterman not noticing me, and put my hand in my desk for a pencil. I found a note. A note that told me this day was far from over. I looked down at my fingers still a little shaky from the locker room and still a little orange from the Cheetos that mom had put in my lunch. Up to this point, they were the highlight of my day.

7

The note said: *After school, Mr. Fresh. Don't be late! Slurpees on you!*

What are the odds there would be two traps in one day? No alarms rang in my head, but I did curse myself for telling a few people when allowance day was in the Greatneck house. Slurpee was a 7/11 brand so it would have to be just a regular old slushie. I hoped they had root beer, but my guess was they stuck with the old stand-bys of grape and cherry. The note said, "Don't be late," yet no time was given except after school. These were not people who thrived on detail. I did have one problem. I had no idea where Mr. Fresh was. Nevertheless, I had seen a little

Dora the Explorer in my youth and knew how to get directions.

The note held few other clues. The handwriting looped and swirled in neat cursive circles with big letters. I would call it good clean juvenile penmanship. Adults wrote fast and lazy. Even good adult handwriting looked hurried and used very small tight letters. This was big, swoopy, and perfect. The author took time. This was written by a kid around my age and more importantly it was written by a girl. Somebody had some information or I had a secret admirer. I doubted the latter because those kinds of notes are sweet and syrupy like chocolate chip pancakes smothered in Mrs. Butterworth with layers of whipped cream. I wouldn't know about them personally, but a friend whom I will not name received a bunch from a girl that turned out to be his best friend. It was about that time I had to change schools again. This note was business.

Mr. Fresh was easier to find than Waldo on a blank canvas.

***

I could not believe I hadn't seen it before. Usually in a new town I will canvas the neighborhood with an alley cat's eye looking for odd places and interesting people, but since I found a wazoo full of interest and more odd than an international side show convention the first day at William B.

Travis, I hadn't had a chance to venture out. Two blocks off my tread-worn route to and from school, Mr. Fresh sat, a dingy oasis of five-dollar half-gallons of milk and seventy-five cent penny-candy. This was a convenience store so small the clerk envied the ice cream truck guy, not for his mobility, but workspace.

The sign outside said, "One student at a time in store." A funny concept since no more than one adult could fit in the store unless they wore the same pants. It looked like this meeting would be "Al Fresco" – a term I heard on a late movie one night and asked my mom if the people were going to actually eat Mr. Fresco. This would make them cannibals and the movie suddenly worth watching. She found that terribly funny and spit her tea across the coffee table before telling me that "Al Fresco" meant to eat out-doors. I was seven and liked the cannibal idea better so every time we went out to eat I asked if we could "Eat Al" instead.

I was pondering slushie options when they walked up behind me. There is a funny trick your mind plays when confronted by people you know, but out of the setting in which you know them. They seem like figures from an entirely different life. I once sat 2 booths away from 3 teachers from my old school at 4:30 in an Applebee's, and the numbers must have been playing with my mind. They looked like my teachers, and were wearing their clothes, but were acting like pirates on a long awaited shore leave. I watched them whooping, laughing, and causing their waiter endless trouble for a pittance of a tip. I had never even seen one of them smile let alone heave huge sobs of tearful laughter like unwilling contestants in an endless tickling booth.

Another job of a good detective is to remember that people are rarely one thing. Nevertheless, I did a double take when Kayla and Ralphie walked up together. We were just three blocks from school, but it felt like China or better yet, Pluto.

"Hey, Handy," Kayla said.

"Hey," echoed Ralphie.

The situation rusted my brain tight, and it took me a second to oil my synapse. It was a second too long.

"Handy, Hello," Ralphie bent down to say.

"No. Hi," I said snapping too, "I was zoned out, stuck in a time warp.

"If you are zoned back in," Ralphie said, "I'll have grape."

"I like cherry," Kayla added.

I wasn't one to be totally upstaged so I pulled out three dollars.

"I'll pay," I said, "but I won't fetch." I handed the money to Ralphie and said, "I'll have root beer."

Ralphie looked at me for less than a second before saying, "Grape it is."

Ralphie walked inside, more than filling the one student maximum.

"They don't have root beer," Kayla said, sincerely sad for me. We headed across the cracked parking lot, weeds running in all directions like an ivy road map, and sat on one of two weather-beaten picnic tables that spent more time as pigeon potties than dining spots. Ralphie set down three large slushies.

"Any change?" I asked.

"Actually, Handy, they were three-fifteen with tax, but I covered you."

"I'll get you something special for Valentine's Day," I said.

Kayla was ready to get serious.

"We think it may be time to do something," she said, "and we thought you might have some ideas."

"Ideas, I have loads," I said. "I'm short on facts, and my plans have been as useful as a mime assembly."

I laid out what I knew and what had happened. I showed my bruise, and I shared my thoughts on Kurt Pesterman, the society, and showed them the hall pass from

Zack Brewer. They listened politely with only a few slurps hindering my story. They were not surprised. Now, it was my turn for some answers.

"Who is Mr. Crumblebean?" I started, cutting right to the heart of my confusion.

Kayla responded, "That was Kurt's dummy."

I could see this was going to be a better story then when Stinky Masterson fell into the city sewer system, which is why we called him Stinky.

"His dummy?" I asked.

"You know, a dummy," Kayla repeated. "It sits on your lap and you try not to move your mouth and make it talk."

"A ventriloquist's dummy," I said, getting the picture and already a little creeped out by the image.

"Yes," Kayla continued, "he brought it for the first day of school last year."

"Fifth Grade," I added.

"Yes," Kayla said, "he loved the dummy. He called him Mr. Crumblebean, and he would bring him to school every chance he could. Kurt was hard to be around anyway, but with Mr. Crumblebean he became annoying and creepy."

"My guess," I interrupted, "is that Kurt was already an electron magnet for getting pushed around. Add a Dummy in everybody's face, and bullies would fly in from Scotland for a chance to taunt him."

"Oh, yeah," Ralphie said, "and I was right there with them."

"You weren't that bad," Kayla stepped in. "Brewer and the other class were much harder on him. You never gave him the swirly-thingy or the wedgies."

"What did you do?" I asked.

"Peer pressure, Handy," Ralphie started. "It even affects bullies. It's cool to have the other guys cracking up when you put someone down. There's a lot of power. Then they are pushing you to be meaner and meaner, and you end up following along to keep them laughing."

"So, before you know it, you are meaner than you thought possible," I said.

Ralphie paused in acknowledgement of my understanding and continued, "I started saying that the dummy was Kurt's girlfriend and that he should kiss her."

"But you weren't the one who made him kiss Mr. Crumblebean," Kayla threw in to try to soften Ralphie's story.

"Yeah, but I did shove the tater tot in his mouth," Ralphie added.

"Kurt's or the dummy's?" I asked.

"The dummy's," Ralphie replied. "Kurt went ballistic and they had to bring in an ambulance."

"I guess you got in trouble," I said, waiting for the "obvious" fairy to come shove a tater tot in my mouth.

"Two days suspension," Ralphie said. "After that, the complaints poured in every time I opened my mouth or walked across the playground."

"They weren't true?" I asked.

"Yes and no," Raphie said. "Bullying is a hard habit to break, and they make it easy."

"Poor baby," I said more sarcastic than I intended.

"Hey," said Kayla, "Ralphie feels awful about it every-day."

"That's okay, Kayla," Ralphie replied.

I interrupted, "I'm sorry, Ralphie, that was harsh. I would like to know what changed for you."

Ralphie sat quiet for what seemed like one year and said, "Do you know what an epiphany is?"

"What sixth grader doesn't?" I said, "Besides all of them."

I paused for effect then added, "It's a sudden moment of clarity where everything becomes completely clear." Epiphany was the stock and trade of a fine sleuth.

Ralphie trudged on seemingly unimpressed, "My uncle

Brad told it to me after he'd given me a gut bruising claw for suggesting he was too old to beat me in one-on-one. He said I'd have an epiphany in fifteen years, long after I could beat him at everything, when I was playing with my own kids or nephews, that it never mattered who was winning anyway. Then he took the ball, bounced it off my head, and scored a three-pointer."

"What does that mean?" Kayla said falling back into the conversation as if she had hyper-spaced herself back into existence.

"I don't know," said Ralphie. "The guy's a comedian, but I did get 'epiphany'."

"You realized the pain you were causing?" I asked.

"That," Ralphie said, as if caring about others' feelings were the smaller part of this equation, "and I was being called to the principal for raising my hand too fast. Every insult was my fault whether I said it or not. Kurt was having fits if you looked at him in class. Then they found Mr. Crumblebean."

"Found him?" I asked, remembering Kurt had told me he watched Mr. Crumblebean's destruction.

"What was left of him," Ralphie added, as I waited for scary music to play in the background.

"Kurt brought him to school as usual," Kayla began, "and after lunch he began whining about how Mr.

Crumblebean was gone, and he wanted him back. He was saying Ralphie had stolen him and told Mr. Treater he'd seen Ralphie near the coat room before we went out for recess."

"And you did not take Crumblebean," I said, knowing it to be true.

"Nope," Ralphie said.

"Was it found?" I asked, already having suspicions.

"Yes," said Kayla. "His head was on a bench in the boy's locker room. His arms and legs were torn apart and thrown all over the shower room. Mr. Treater brought us all down to look at it, yelled at us for half an hour, and the boy's locker room really smells bad. How do you guys go in there?"

Ignoring the last comment I said, "That's when the whole society thing started and the cage."

"No, it took the rest of the year for the Agitator's Awareness Society to be created, and the cage started the first week of this year," Kayla said.

"Who do you think whacked Crumblebean?" I asked.

"No one knows," Kayla said for both of them.

"Do you think Kurt did it himself?"

"Maybe," Kayla said.

"Who's in the Agitator's Awareness Society?"

"I tried to get in," Kayla said, "but by the time I heard about it, it was already formed."

"How does that happen?" I said confused.

"You know how schools work," Kayla said. "The teachers and principal put together the kids they chose, add the rules, tell the rest of us later, and pretend we were all partners."

"Wait," I was stunned like a deer in a searchlight, "Mrs. Austin told me Kurt put the Society together after meeting with students, and you all came up with the plan."

"We all knew Kurt was the head of the Society," Ralphie said, "but we thought the school put it together and chose Kurt."

"Who do you give your complaints to?" I asked.

"In the box," Kayla said. "You've seen it in the hall. We know kids who have complained about bullying. The rumor is that if you put one in the box you suddenly start getting in trouble, and your complaint disappears. But, no one now admits to complaining."

"How is it that Kurt Pesterman gets to sign hall passes?"

"It's what they call peer-to-peer help," Kayla said. "After Kurt was carted off, the school was going to be sued and some psychologist came in to help us deal with the trauma."

"The trauma of a tater tot stuffed in a dummy's mouth," I said, wondering which Twilight Zone I'd stepped into.

"Hey, kids have been expelled at schools because somebody brings a plastic knife in a lunch box," Ralphie drawled out.

Kayla continued her speech, "The psychologist lady's solution was to make Kurt the head of the peer-to-peer help group. Turns out she is Kurt's mom's cousin. If another student felt like he was going to 'lose it' from the stress of..." Kayla paused and looked at Ralphie.

"Me," Ralphie tossed out.

"Then they can go talk to Kurt," Kayla said. "If they really are wigging out, Kurt can give them a stress pass for the counselor or nurse to take a 'stress time-out'."

"This is crazy, even for teachers," I said. "Kurt is in total control of every kid in the school, and if he needs some muscle to knock someone straight, he writes a pass and the brute squad delivers a message."

"And," Kayla said, "he is the only one to complain to, which is why we decided to get your help, Handy. We need some fresh ideas."

"I'm thinking, instead of going into the cage," I said with only a little bit of sarcasm.

"Funny," said Ralphie.

"What we need to do," I said, "is make Kurt sweat a little, get him in the open, and caught in the act."

"The act of what?" Kayla asked. "He's the victim."

"He doesn't know I've got a hall pass of his, and he has to communicate with his thugs somewhere. I've got to get him to slip up."

"You've got to?" Ralphie asked. "What about us? What do we do?"

"Nothing," I said. "You step so far away from this that you start speaking Swedish."

"What?" Ralphie said.

"Don't do anything," I said. "Kayla, you too, I mean it! I have the beginnings of a plan, and a purple tongue from this grape slushie. I need to get my mouth washed out with some IBC and line up my ducks so straight that when they quack all you hear is ruffled butt feathers. Any extra players will cause it to cave in. Kurt has to feel I'm working alone, and if you two start getting in trouble, the whole thing will fall apart. So, promise."

They sat. They sipped. They exchanged looks.

"Okay, Handy," Ralphie said, "we will. But if you need us, we are there for you."

"Thanks," I said.

"What will you do first?" Kayla asked.

"It's time I registered a complaint with the Agitator's Awareness Society and caused them some agitation."

8

I dropped my complaint into the AAS box first thing Monday morning. I needed at least three days preparation before I could put any plan into action. The complaint took three hours of tweaking to get it just the way I wanted. It had to sound sincere, but also be an obvious challenge to Kurt. Mine said that I was ready to take Kurt on in his own arena and play his game because this note was going to bring this fight to me. I had to be ready to adjust to whatever Mr. Pesterman and his Society had to dish out.

My dad asked me what I was working on, and it might surprise most kids to know I told him the entire story. I figured my parents needed to know the possibilities of harm to my academic career, and they might need to be prepared to take a personal day or two off from work to listen to the principal speak unkindly about their precious boy detective. I had no idea how devious or dirty Kurt would play.

Dad's response, "We trust you Sport, and we will be there for you." I had an epiphany. When it came to parents, I was as lucky as Mowgli from *Jungle Book*. *Jungle Book II* that is, not the first *Jungle Book*. Although, who wouldn't want to be raised by wolves for a while?

Dad also told me to consider the consequences and asked if I wanted him and Mom to talk to my teacher.

"Yes and no," I replied.

"Okay, Sport," he said. "Decide, though, if the problems you can cause for yourself are worth the good you can accomplish."

"Can't help it Dad," I said, as I looked into his knowing eyes. I worried for a second that he was going to hug me, but he faked the hug, grabbed the Nerf ball, and put up a three-pointer from the doorway. Nothing but net.

***

I waited as long as I could, near, but out of sight from the complaint box for Kurt, or someone, to pick up the note. No one came. I walked into homeroom wondering how long I would have to wait for my bitter little pill to give

Kurt a stomach ache. Already, the waiting wasn't doing anything for my appetite. Bully victims often have the same feelings. The time you spend worrying about the couple of minutes a day you have to spend crossing the bully's path, makes your nerves a wreck for hours or days. I wasn't crazed with anticipation, but I do prefer the action to begin rather than the wait. I didn't wait long.

Kurt walked in and eyeballed me harder than a copper to a kleptomaniac. I pulled my lips back in a smile so tight oxygen atoms had to knock on my mouth to enter and let me breathe. Kurt strolled by the other students, who either physically or mentally moved away from him like a pit viper in a cuddly bunny's burrow.

"Mr. Greatneck," Kurt said as he slithered up. "It seems we have a problem."

"Oh, good you got my note," I said, innocent as peach fuzz on a baby's forehead.

"Note?" Kurt said, looking up and right, "I didn't get a note." This was lying.

"I've been hearing rumors that you are harassing some of the smaller fourth graders," he said.

"Weak ruse, Pesterman," I said calmly and politely knowing Kurt would know what a ruse was. "You have no complaints about me, and I'm spotless. You run to the teachers with this garbage and they will laugh you out of your goofy plaid pants. Even if you get a fourth grader to lie, and you can't, I can prove I haven't been around them enough to make threats. Furthermore," I said, making sure my voice was still as friendly as Mr. Rogers on good neighbor day, "I've already made friends with eighty percent of this school. They might be scared of you, but they won't lie for you. And, your thugs crying 'Bully' will sound a tad hollow since I am half their size."

Kurt stood and mulled over my words. He also seemed to be waiting for something. He knew his threats were useless, but he was letting me know the game had begun, and waiting for some sort of signal. His sign received, he went into action. I had to move quickly or lose round one.

"Well, Greatneck," Kurt said as he looked over my shoulder toward the door for the seventh time. "You may be right about that, so I guess I need to take matters into my own hands."

Kurt had positioned himself uncomfortably close to me between the desks while we talked. Before I could peel myself away from the stench of his pop-tart breath, he jumped backwards over the desk and threw all his books into the air. The scream that came from his mouth as he fell, tore through the classroom like ice-pick-sharp nails on a blackboard.

I knew Kurt's play in an instant. I had about three seconds to mount my counter attack. Glancing over my shoulder, I saw what Kurt was waiting to happen. He had timed his move perfectly.

He flipped like a rag doll seconds after Mrs. Austin came in the room. Worse yet, for me, Ralphie lumbered in a few seconds before Mrs. Austin. The whole class was watching him, and could not verify Kurt's Olympic vault over the desk. Kurt wanted it to be my word against his, and he knew most calls go to the home team. Luckily, Kurt wasn't playing the B-team today, but reigning state champs. As he fell, I went into action. I ran around his falling form and slammed my books on the bookshelf below the window, thanking fate that it was a warm day and the window was open. The boom of my books startled everyone more than Kurt's wounded baby lamb cries. The room and even Kurt went silent.

"Boys, what's going on over here?" Mrs. Austin asked.

Kurt's lip began to quiver like Jell-O in an earthquake.

"Greatneck just pushed me over that desk," he said looking around the room for sympathy. There was none to be had from his classmates as this song had dropped off the charts. Everyone backed away to what seemed like a safe distance from any lose involvement that might still be flying around the room.

"Is this true, Hannibal?" Mrs. Austin asked looking perplexed and disappointed. I let the accusation hang in the air like the sheet when Mom flaps it over the bed and it floats down over the mattress. This sheet was not coming down to smother me.

"Yes," I said, and if a word could steal the power of speech from an entire room, I found the word. Mrs. Austin looked surprised. Kurt went pale. He'd expected me to start stammering trying to deny his fake tattle, then he could use his credibility to force the issue, call me a liar, and bring a great deal of suspicion my way. Denial always looks guilty.

"You did push Kurt?" Mrs. Austin asked, stuck in a time warp. "Yes," I repeated, "and way harder than I intended."

"You wanted to push him then?" Mrs. Austin asked. She was getting this picture slower than if I were sky-writing it.

"That wasp was huge," I said, "and with Kurt allergic to bee stings, I figured I needed to get him out of the way fast. I didn't mean to push him that hard, though. Are you okay, Kurt?" My mock sincerity was first rate.

Kurt was speechless. His mouth gaped open like a small bass in a Chinese restaurant pond. Mrs. Austin's brain finally joined the party. She said, "Oh, that's why you hit your books on the shelf."

Kurt tried to recover, but it was too late.

"But he said he was sick of me."

This recovery was too little too late.

"Why would I say 'me,' Kurt?" I said looking at Kurt as if he were a silly pants. "I said bee. Although, actually, it was a wasp."

I picked up my books and there was, of course, no wasp.

"Looks like he flew out the window," I said.

"Well, it is a good thing you were here, Handy," said Mrs. Austin. I was Handy again. Kurt lost this round and he gave up like a four-pound fish on a hundred-pound test line.

"Yeah, I guess," he said with the sincerity of a wicked stepmother.

"A little fall is better than swelling up like a balloon. Right Kurt?" said Mrs. Austin.

"Thank you," Kurt said through vise-like clenched teeth. He paused and said the next word as if he were swallowing a booger sandwich, "Handy."

I could see that hurt, and I know this was just the beginning. The commotion waning, we all moved to our seats, and Kurt picked up his books as no one felt like helping. As I walked by the cage, Ralphie asked, "How did you know Kurt was allergic to bee stings?"

"How could he not be?" I said. "And, I was in the nurse's office for lice check and saw an Epi-Pen with his name on it. Detectives should notice everything."

"What do you write with that?" Ralphie asked. I was going to explain that an Epi-Pen was not a Pen. It was an emergency shot that anyone who has severe allergies needs to have on hand at all times in case they are, for example, stung by a bee, but I couldn't be seen loitering around Ralphie's cage so I just said, "Epiphanies Ralphie. I used it to write an Epi-phany."

9

Kurt was not going to underestimate me again. I knew he was plotting because he never raised his hand in class again that day, and for a know-it-all like Kurt to resist being the center of all knowledge was akin to a wolf deciding cabbage was a better food choice. He sat muttering to himself like the homeless man downtown that talks to Elvis all day. Why old crazy people always talk to Elvis, I will never figure out. People under twenty hardly know who Elvis is anymore. I wondered to whom my generation was going to mumble that night, as I was writing my fifth complaint to the Agitator's Awareness Society. I ended up writing Hillary Duff instead of Zack Brewer before snapping myself back to reality. Sometimes multi-tasking is not the answer.

Everyday I put a new complaint in the box, and nothing had been done, positively or negatively. I knew I was getting under Kurt's skin because he was stewing about like a stray dog after 29 ½ days in the pound. Zack Brewer and his friend also had me on their radar. I'm no psychic, but I could tell Kurt's thugs were privy to what my notes said about them because their ignoring of me bordered on contempt.

I needed to spur him into action, so this complaint said I would take my grievance to the principal's office if I did not see any action soon. "Be ready Handy," I thought as I put the note and copies of all the other notes in my bag. I might need them as evidence soon.

I fought off my root beer cravings, and I hopped in the sack to get a mountain of rest. Tomorrow might be a long day.

The next morning slipped by without incident and a 98% on the geography quiz on state capitols. This case was causing my grades to suffer. I switched Bismarck with Pierre and Concord with Montpelier, a rookie mistake. At least I didn't put St. Louis down for Missouri like sixty-percent of the class. I also avoided Kayla and Ralphie, which hurt even more now because I knew them. Wasting time not having good friends was a lonely business. I missed hanging out with them even when I was buying the slurpies.

Always being on guard is tiring, and maybe Kurt knew that, too. His plan may have been to wait for me to show a little weakness, then he could pounce. Gym ended as usual and I was the first one in the locker room to pick up my backpack. The rest of the class filed in as I was opening the lock that kept my bag from more homework-nappers. No one else used locks because thievery was virtually non-existent at William B. Travis, but I justified it to questions by saying that one homework prank on me was enough.

The scream pierced the locker room like an air horn in a pup tent. Crying bellowed forth next with sobs so deep I didn't know if penguins could hold their breath so long. I ran toward the cries and pushed my way through the amass-ing smelly sixth grade boy gawk-fest. It was Anson Summerhead digging at his eyes as if they'd just seen his grandma in her underwear by mistake and wanted out of his head.

"What's wrong?" I screamed as I bent down to try to look into his eyes. No luck, Anson was hysterical with pain. I looked around at the throng of frightened students.

"Anyone see what happened?" I asked.

"He just put on his glasses and started screaming," I heard from behind my back.

Anson Summerhead was serious about his glasses, or more correct to say, his parents were serious about him never breaking his glasses. He always changed into those hard plastic sports glasses that make you look like a paint ball target for gym class so his good pair would not catch a dodge ball seconds before his face did.

Anson continued to scream and I said, "Hold on, buddy."

I picked up Anson's glasses and liquid ran down the lenses as if someone had sprayed 409 all over them. I smelled it and it was not 409.

"Help me get him to the shower," I said. "Now!"

I handed Anson's glasses to Ralphie.

"Don't lose those or wipe them off."

Jaden Franks grabbed Anson's other arm and we dragged him to the shower.

"Go get the nurse!" I yelled as someone ran from the room. We dumped Anson under the water, and I held his head up to let the water pour into his blazing eyes.

"You're gonna be okay," I said to Anson. He was still bawling, but you could see the water's easing effect like the first steps into the ocean after crossing a sea of burning sand.

"What's going on here, Mr. Greatneck?" the nurse said running into the room.

"Someone sprayed mace onto Anson's glasses," I said, "Ralphie."

Ralphie produced the glasses.

"How do you know what mace is, Hannibal?" she asked.

"I toured a police station last year," I said. "My uncle is the captain. I even saw a demonstration of the use of mace, and this is the same effect. At first, I thought it was glass cleaner, which would sting, but pepper spray would hurt a great deal more with just the mist getting in the eyes. I knew I needed to rinse his eyes, and since it was not sprayed into his eyes, it was easier to clear. Unlike glass cleaner, mace has no real lasting effects."

The nurse pulled Anson from the shower still in pain, but no longer hysterical. He now looked like a drenched cat with severe allergy problems.

"It's a good thing you were here, Mr. Greatneck," the nurse said, heading Anson up the stairs as the class filed out. The shower soaked Anson, but I had only gotten my sleeve and pant legs wet, so not needing new clothes, I paused for a second to consider who might profit from this assault. If they were trying to frame me, this stunk worse than a cable showing of *Ernest Goes To Camp*. I was the first one back to the locker room, but had no time to get out Anson's glasses, spray them, and hide the mace. If Kurt or his raiding party did this, they were taking criminal, reform-school-type chances.

Everyone was half way back to class as I picked up my backpack and headed up the stairs to class. Furthermore, I thought, how could Kurt think anyone would think I would put mace on someone's glasses? The nurse said it was good that I was around, and I am always the first to help.

"Arrrrgh!" I yelled in my head with an epiphany that snapped my brain stem in two. Of course, Kurt knew I'd be the first to help. It was a diversion. Yikes! I pulled open my backpack. I never call myself stupid, but dunderhead fit very well.

There was nothing new in the main compartment, but all the copies of my complaints were gone.

"Great," I thought.

This was not part of their plan to take some copies of evidence, they wouldn't even know was there. This was a small gift from me. I kept searching. There was nothing in the pockets. Then, bingo, tada, and hello, I checked the padding in-between the shoulder straps and the main compartment and found a plastic knife. Was it irony that just a week before, Kayla, Ralphie, and I were discussing plastic knives in connection with suspension? Since we hadn't studied irony yet, and I only knew the word from an old song my cousin liked, I moved my mind to other matters. Matters like the fact that Zack Brewer was coming out of the principal's office with the principal. It didn't take a nuclear scientist to figure out where they were going.

I jumped back down the stairs into the locker room. This place was causing me all sorts of trouble this year. I had less than a minute to figure out a solution. In my favor was a principal that walked with the gait of a three-legged turtle. I looked around quick. Kurt was smart, because if I simply threw it away or tried to hide it, then an extensive search of the locker room would put a great deal of suspicion on me. Add that to Zack's made-up eye witness account of seeing me put the knife in my bag, and all my complaints vanished as evidence of their frame, and I was looking as guilty as the cookie monster in Oreo village.

"Think fast, Handy," I muttered.

"That your backpack?"

The voice surprised me like a roach jumping out of a box of candy. It was the janitor.

"Is that your backpack?" he asked again slower, as he noticed the plastic knife in my hand. "Where did you get that?"

"It was in my backpack," I said, still trying to come up with a plan.

"Oh, that's why that other boy was over here while everyone one else was in the shower," he said.

"Which boy?" I asked.

"One of the two who was picking on you the other day," he said.

"Did you see him put it in?" I asked, a small glimmer of hope flashing across my face.

"No," he said, "I came in late and just saw him set it down and walk away. I could tell the principal that much."

"Thank you," I said, "but that's not good enough."

"You get caught with that, and you are going to be in big trouble," he said, as he pulled out his troll head key chain and shook it at me before selecting the key to lock up the boiler room. "It'd be sad to see you expelled after the way you helped that other boy. Sorry, I didn't see enough to get you off the hook."

The answer hit me like an iceberg, and I turned to the janitor with a question only he could answer.

"Do you have any glue?"

***

I do not like to call myself a genius, but luck mixed with a touch of panic can be the path to inspiration. The janitor's door had just closed him into the boiler room; I was still zipping up my pack, when Principal Perryman and Zack Brewer came in.

"Mr. Greatneck," Principal Perryman said, with the serious voice adults use when they want your name to substitute for shut up, stop it, or how dare you, "will you please open your backpack?"

"Sure," I said stalling a second to see if Zack would pipe up and annoy the principal. He did not disappoint.

"I saw him put it in there," Zack blurted out excited to hurry this up to the part where I get in trouble.

"Mr. Brewer," Principal Perryman said, "I will handle this."

"I'm sorry," I said. "What did you see?"

"The knife!" Zack practically screamed, pointing to my backpack as if there were some confusion as to which backpack we were talking about, and to emphasize the fact he was nervous and had nothing to do with his hands.

"That is enough, Mr. Brewer!" the principal said. Zack wasn't annoying; he was making the principal angry.

"Mr. Greatneck," he continued, "please open your backpack."

I stood for a second acting confused then put a wide smile on my face.

"Oh, I get it," I said as I opened my bag and reached deep inside.

I have never seen a man as fast with glue and a pair of tin snips as the janitor. Within seconds of telling him my idea, he grabbed the plastic knife, cut off the blade, threw it in the boiler room, yanked out a tube of super glue, decapitated his key chain, and glued his oversized troll head on the knife handle.

When I pulled it out of the backpack already dry, Zack deflated faster than a Macy's Thanksgiving Day balloon at an archery contest.

"He must have seen the handle of my art project," I said, handing the odd craft to the principal. "There's no blade, but it is a plastic knife handle. Art is not my best thing. I know this looks kind of like a Trollpop, but Zack saw the handle when I put it in the bag. I can see where he might be concerned. I should have thought of that, and informed the office at the start of school."

"Yes, Mr. Greatneck," said Principal Perryman, handing me back the troll-on-a-stick as if it offended his artistic sensibilities, but not his safety ones, "but this isn't a problem. Sorry, to have bothered you, now both of you get back to your classes."

"Sorry to worry you, Zack," I said and smirked at him. "You were very brave to bring this to the attention of the principal."

I walked ahead to Principal Perryman.

"Sir, may I go to the nurse's office?" I asked, leaving Zack to ponder his failure, slink back to Kurt to repent, and possibly watch Kurt's face burn a brilliant red.

10

Anson was sitting in a puddle in the nurse's office his eyes stinging, but the pain was bearable. The nurse was on the phone with one of the Summerhead parents.

"Yes, please come down right away and we will explain further," she said. "No his glasses were not broken, but he will need to see his doctor right away. His eyes are swollen and red, but he should be fine... No, his glasses are fine. Okay, after school then. Goodbye."

A stab of sadness for Anson swept through me and not for the mace in his eyes.

"Mr. Greatneck," the nurse said, "you did a great job today."

"Thanks, Handy," Anson threw in slowly between sniffs.

"I hear pepper spray can really clear the sinuses," I said, trying to raise Anson's spirits.

"Do you know who might have done this?" the nurse asked.

In a normal school or situation, I would have related my suspicions, but this was as normal as a haunted house on Christmas. Kurt still had the power and would have had his lackeys do the dirty work. He was getting desperate, though. His failure meant Kurt would have to up the ante and risk exposing his entire operation to stop me. Telling the nurse the truth now would be as useful as showing UFO magazine pictures of stomped down corn in a circle and screaming about how the aliens abducted you. They would print it, but no one would really believe you.

"I couldn't tell you," I said, technically not a lie, but I made it sound as if I didn't know. "Maybe somebody who didn't know how much damage it would cause."

"I thought we'd cleaned up these kinds of problems?" the nurse said.

Anson and I both shook our heads. The nurse figured we were agreeing with her. We knew it was pity for her ignorance and our future.

I got a pass back to class and walked into Mrs. Austin's room, still a little damp and anticipating the faces of my classmates. I knew they were talking about the incident already. I slipped in the door to hear Mrs. Austin telling how dangerous pranks can be, and she hoped the guilty party would turn themselves in to spare themselves extended suspension or worse. I handed her my pass and felt every eye follow me to my seat as if my wet limbs were really on fire.

Mrs. Austin finished her speech and waited, as if the villain would suddenly leap up and confess for the good of William B. Travis and the men of the Alamo. I will never understand how many times a tactic has to not work before teachers will give it up.

No one made a sound.

The silence became as uncomfortable as when my cousin comes to grandma's house for Christmas and tells dirty jokes around the table. No response forthcoming, Mrs. Austin told us to read or do homework until the end of class. Kayla went to the front of the room to talk to Mrs. Austin, and slipped a note under my book on the way back to her desk.

It said: "Same time. Same place, & my allowance."

11

"It's too much, Handy," Kayla said as we sipped our slurpies on the weathered pigeon potty that doubled as a picnic bench near Mr. Fresh. "You could have gotten expelled."

Ralphie piped in, "And the fact Kurt doesn't care who gets hurt means he will try anything. It's time to pull back and ride out the year, man."

I knew they'd be stunned when I weaved my tale of locker room excitement with the janitor, the troll head, Zack, the plastic knife, and their connection with Anson

Summerhead. I didn't know they would be worried enough about me to want to stop. It felt good.

"I get you, but even if I wanted to stop, I couldn't," I said. "Kurt won't stop until he silences me, and the only way to do that is by getting me in trouble. My credibility is higher than ever, and Kurt is seething with hate and fear. A master mind in meltdown is ripe to slip ups, and I told you I have a plan."

"Or, he will hurt someone else and find a way to pin it on you," Kayla added. Kayla's eyes looked as scared as a Chihuahua in a pit bull pen making her even cuter. I felt puberty knocking at my knees.

"I don't think Kurt is going to hurt anyone else," I said.

"You mean you think he's going to bring the fight right to you," Ralphie said. "Maybe, you need a little help, Handy. I could make sure Brewer knows it would be better if he kept his hands to himself."

"Ralphie," I said, thinking I might just cry if I wasn't a hard-boiled detective, "the fact you want to is great, but you," I looked at Kayla, "both of you have to stay farther away from this than my sweet tooth to pickle cake. This will fall apart faster than wet toilet paper if you guys jump in now. No matter how much you want to help, or feel I am in trouble, you need to watch from the sidelines."

They sat there quiet wondering what to say. I spoke before anything came to them.

"I will make you a deal," I said. "If this isn't over in two days, we will all walk into the principal's office and tell our stories, and take our chances that he will believe us over Kurt. If my plan works, we won't have to."

"If it doesn't work," Ralphie said, "you'll be shipped off to a reality show teen boot camp and it won't matter."

We sat and alternately got brain freeze.

Kayla said, "Handy, why do you have to say stuff like pickle cake and toilet paper?"

12

> Meet me in the speech room.
>
> At the start of recess.
>
> So I can tell you the truth.
>
> Handy

First, the author used an inkjet printer, probably one from the school's computer lab, which was a place with so little supervision that a small online auction business selling stolen pencils could be run by enterprising students. The speech room was a nice touch. It was an awful lonely place during recess. The note said the start of recess, meaning unless a playground monitor suddenly became interested in his or her duty no one would miss us for twenty odd minutes.

The last clue on this note was a touch of brilliance. It was signed, Handy.

It was a typed signature, but effective. No matter what happened at this little party, Kurt could say I sent the invitation. A little voice told me to spend this recess playing kickball, and wait for a chance that looked less like my Alamo. Walking into this situation was crazier than riding the Zipper after three corn dogs and an elephant ear. They both made my stomach turn, but at least the Zipper is an awesome ride pre-barf.

As the bell rang, I winked at Kayla, smirked at Ralphie, and told my little voice to save me a spot on third base. I couldn't pass up such a well-executed set-up. Curiosity killed the cat, as they say, but I had only used up two lives, so far, and I wanted to see if I was serving snacks.

***

It wasn't the voice inside my head that I heard as I neared the speech room door. Kurt was not alone. Kurt's plan was A+ so far. The hallway on my walk from Mrs. Austin's room was as lonely as a water park in December. I've seen halls less abandoned during fire drills.

"Just calm down," a voice broke through the door sharp, high, whiny. "He'll show up." It was Kurt.

I walked in. There were no snacks. I seemed to be a terrible host.

"Of course, I'm here," I said, "I got a note from me, telling me I wanted me to be here. I have to find out what I want."

"Shut up, Goofyneck!" Zack Brewer spit out.

"Zack, sit down, and be quiet!" Kurt spit back. "I'm sorry, Mr. Greatneck. You know Zack is slow and hot headed."

"It's hard to find intelligent bullies who work cheap," I said.

"Funny," said Kurt. "See, we could be friends Mr. Greatneck."

"Sure," I said.

"Welcome to the Agitator's Awareness Society," Kurt said spreading his arms around the room. "Our mission is to keep William B. Travis Elementary School safe."

"For you," I cut in.

"For everybody," he said.

"And anyone who disagrees gets a bully call from Zack and…" I stopped my speech. "I'm sorry," I said to Zack's partner, "What is your name?"

We all stood silent for a moment as nameless Thug

Two stood confused as to why I was talking to him and not Kurt, or his name had slipped his mind, too.

"Uh, Jack," he said as if he'd never said it before and it sounded oddly foreign to him.

"Jack, what?" I asked, as if I was interviewing him for a temp position in an office cubical.

Jack's brain leaped back to the situation at hand, and the realization that we were not friends. He was here to intimidate me, or worse.

"Jack Sh-," he started to say as Kurt drowned him out with an indignant scream.

"Mr. Greenblatt!" Kurt yapped, "That is enough."

My new friend, Jack Greenblatt, slunk back to his post amply disciplined.

"Alright, Kurt," I said, "why are we here?"

"First things first, Hannibal," said Kurt, as if my first name smelled funny. "Zack, take his bag."

Zack moved toward me fast as Jack slid over and blocked the door. Zack reached out and grabbed my backpack. I fought just enough to make him fall over backward when I let go. Kurt and Jack cracked up. It's unendingly interesting that the bullies and the villains in every story even like to see their comrades fail and get hurt. Evil has no compassion, even for friends.

"You think you're funny, Goofyneck?" Zack said, as he pulled his embarrassed rear end off the floor.

"Zack," said Kurt exasperated, "that was your own fault, and stop saying, Goofyneck. It's insipid, and Mr. Greatneck is our guest."

"What's insipid mean?" Zack asked, as he straightened out his dignity.

"Stupid," I said. Zack glared at me, and Jack for the second time was looking as if he felt left out.

"Boring," Kurt corrected me, "juvenile, not clever." Kurt turned his attention like a hungry mouser back in my direction. I spoke first.

"Do all the guests of the Agitator's Awareness Society have their bags taken from them by force?"

"You are our first guest, Mr. Greatneck," Kurt said, as his pathetic yellow teeth peaked out to show me a nauseating little smile.

"An honor, I'm sure," I said.

"We need to make a small trade with you," Kurt went on. "Zack, if you please."

Zack handed him my bag, and Kurt dug through it carefully as if I were carrying a small snake with a taste for bologna colored skin.

"Aha," said Kurt as he pulled out Zack's hall pass from the front pocket. "Sloppy, Hannibal," he said, proud of his first point in our little game. "I would have kept this elsewhere."

"How did you know I had the hall pass you gave Zack so they could threaten me?" I asked.

"I asked Zack to return it to me after they messed up your little talk," Kurt said. "I watched him search his pockets for five minutes like a brain-dead baboon. They told me you tried to attack them, and that is not your style. I realized you must have taken it."

"Very smart, Kurt," I said. "You tell them to punch me, too?"

"No," Kurt said. "I hate violence unless it is absolutely necessary. Your actions confused their pea brains."

I looked at Jack and Zack, "And you guys let him talk about you that way?" They stood quiet and started looking at the floor like naughty kittens whose mittens were long since missing.

"They know who is in charge, Mr. Greatneck," Kurt said, "and I hope you will come around to understanding what they understand. I can get you a lot of perks around school, or I can get you expelled."

"By pushing yourself over a desk?" I asked.

"That was a feeble attempt on my part," Kurt said with a glint of respect for me in his beady eye. "It would have worked on any other student."

"I'm just a humble public servant," I said.

"You are a huge annoyance," Kurt shot back, "but a worthy one. The troll head on the plastic knife handle was sheer genius."

"Putting mace in Anson Summerhead's glasses was sadistic," I said.

Zack and Jack were having trouble following along already, but when I said sadistic their faces showed visible confusion. Kurt noticed.

"Sadistic!" he screamed at them. "It means that I enjoyed hurting Mr. Summerhead."

Zack and Jack nodded their heads like they knew something about hurting people and its intrinsic joys.

"See, Mr. Greatneck," said Kurt, "we are a lot alike. Our vocabularies are high school level, or higher. We are both reading at a tenth grade level. Our math scores make these two look like Neanderthals."

Zack and Jack took no offense to the suggestion they were sub-human because they must have thought Neanderthal was a pro-wrestler.

Kurt blathered on, "We could do a lot together like Jedi Knights, and I used mace on Anson Summerhead because I knew it wouldn't cause lasting harm."

"You're a prince," I said.

"Okay, I'm giving you a chance, Mr. Greatneck," Kurt

swallowed. "Handy. It's a chance to stop sending complaints, and even join the society."

I stood thinking how much fun it would be playing Star Wars at Kurt's house, and thanking my lucky stars that it was before lunch and my stomach was empty, so I had nothing to throw up.

"I'd like to know something first," I said.

"Anything," Kurt replied.

"What happened to Mr. Crumblebean?"

Kurt showed the first sign of emotion since we began our tea party.

"Some sacrifices must be made," he said looking as though he may start crying. "I had to have Zack do it. It was a great loss. Everybody loved Mr. Crumblebean."

Zack and Jack both rolled their eyes.

Kurt was oblivious and continued, "As my mom said, 'It was for the greater good.'"

"Your mother knows what you've been up to?" I asked.

"Of course, where would I get mace?" Kurt replied as if I were an idiot for not seeing this before. "It's from her "self-defense for women" kit. No one pushes her around. She does not want me to be like my dad who left after she called him a spineless wimp. She was always screaming at him that he was a wuss and useless. I'd hear her yelling from my room all the time. I didn't like Anson getting hurt, and having Mr. Crumblebean destroyed was awful, but it was for the greater good."

Kurt stopped his speech and looked a little smaller than his pint-size self. I had to poke myself in the cerebrum with a figurative finger by thinking, "Don't feel sorry for Kurt Pesterman. Don't feel sorry for Kurt Pesterman."

Kurt regrouped and said, "My mother wants you destroyed, but I'm giving you a chance to play along. If you don't want to, then I said I was trading you for something."

Kurt pulled the mace out of his pocket and held it up.

"When they find this in your backpack, it will look like you sprayed Anson's glasses to be a hero."

"No one's going to believe that," I said. "I didn't have time to do it, and haven't touched that mace."

"This is sixth grade, Mr. Greatneck," Kurt said. "No one is going to check for fingerprints, and any explanation that means less work for them, will destroy you at this school. And we have another surprise that will seal the deal for your doom."

Kurt was starting to sound like every classic movie villain.

Kurt nodded at Zack who nodded back, and grabbed me around my arms and held me vise tight. I looked up at Jack who was cracking his knuckles.

"No one is going to believe the mace set-up if you beat

me like a piñata," I said.

"Very true," Kurt said, "but you think very small, Greatneck."

Kurt nodded to Jack who practically jumped up and down with excitement, but instead of coming at me, he placed himself in front of Kurt.

Kurt's plan, or more accurately, Kurt's mom's plan punched me harder than Zack could have.

I screamed, "No, Kurt! This is crazy! Don't let him hit you!"

Kurt wasn't listening. He began to shake and closed his eyes. When he spoke the fear spilled out along with the words.

"Okay, Jack," Kurt managed to sputter out between his growing sobs. Jack's eyes beamed as he warmed up his fists.

I screamed at the top of my lungs, "Help! Teacher! Fire! Anyone!"

It was no use, the halls were still empty and recess was in full swing. I tried to fight to free myself from Zack's grip. He squeezed tighter and dropped his whole weight on me like a bag of potatoes. We smashed to the floor and I looked up. Kurt was mumbling, "It's for the greater good. I am not spineless."

The punching started.

13

If my screams didn't attract attention, Kurt's banshee style shrieks would. Jack looked thrilled to beat on Kurt.

Kurt lay on the floor crying so loud he made Anson's blubbering look like a wince.

Zack held me tight and looked up at Jack who was panting with adrenaline.

"Go," Zack said.

Jack ran from the room, and Zack began to count.

"One, two, three, four."

Kurt covered his eyes and wailed. Zack hit the number thirty; we could hear footsteps running up the hall. Kurt's mom had planned this to the second. Zack let me go and ran out of the door that leads into an adjoining classroom. I got up and went to Kurt. There was blood on the floor and he had lost a tooth. His eyes were already swelling up. The door swung open hard and the nurse rushed in followed by Jack.

"Oh, my heavens," she said rushing down to Kurt. "What have you done Mr. Greatneck?"

I stood silent looking at Jack, a new disrespect for these kinds of punks.

"Go wait in the principal's office, Mr. Greatneck," the nurse said snapping me back to the present and my situation. Talking was useless at this point. I grabbed my backpack and started for the door.

"Bag," Kurt sputtered out between sobs a smattering of blood coming from his mouth. He was playing all his cards.

"What?" said the nurse.

"Bag," Kurt said again, as if that one word hurt more than Jack's fists.

"Mr. Greatneck, let me see your backpack," the nurse said holding out her hand like I was going to hand over my spleen. I handed it over without question. She opened it and pulled out the small can of mace.

"This is outrageous, Mr. Greatneck," she said, as if she had arrested the Easter Bunny for throwing eggs at a nun.

"I'll hold on to this." She went on, "You go to the office."

I left with a passing glance at Jack whose eyes danced with joy. I was destroyed; he got to punch somebody, and was finally an important player in this criminal enterprise.

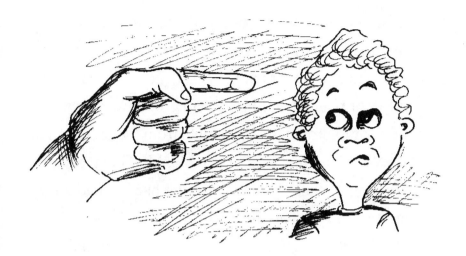

14

I sat in the inner sanctum of the principal's office, meaning right by his desk, alone for the next two hours listening to the flurry of activity outside the door at the secretary's desk and office waiting area. I heard the secretary calling my parents. Which parent she spoke to, I don't know. They were both on their way down. I heard Kurt's mom come in in a blustering tirade of dirty words and threats of lawsuits.

I wondered if she practiced these speeches or was she a natural bully. Whichever it was, I could tell she enjoyed being mad. If I didn't already know she had created this whole situation, I might be irate along with her. The other thing that kept me off her side was that she was verbally attacking me – yelling that I was a manic and better be expelled or better yet sent to jail.

The door opened and Principal Perryman came in and shut the door to drown out the shouts from the outer office.

"You are in a great deal of trouble, Mr. Greatneck," he said like a man whose life was circling back to bad after a nice vacation in Pleasantville.

"It looks that way," I said trying to sound humble.

Principal Perryman did a double take as if my words were another language.

"Mr. Greatneck," he said as serious as a cancer diagnosis, "you are looking at more than suspension. Mrs. Pesterman wants me to contact the police. Your parents will be here in about twenty minutes, and we will all meet with Kurt and his mother. Unless your story is more convincing than the evidence this could destroy many years of your life. I will have to call the police, and you will be arrested, even though you are a minor.

"Twenty minutes?" I said.

***

When the twenty minutes were up and my parents walked in looking worried but unsurprised, I had not convinced the principal to call off the police. They were still on their way.

Mom and Dad greeted Principal Perryman and sat on both sides of me like emperor penguins shielding their baby from the frigid Antarctic cold, and Mrs. Pesterman was a blizzard.

The door burst open and Mrs. Pesterman entered the room in a whirlwind of accusations. The principal stood up and Kurt limped in aided by the nurse. Mrs. Pesterman showed about as much concern for her son as an alligator for a chicken egg.

"Where are the police?" Mrs. Pesterman screamed in the principal's face.

"Calm down, please," Principal Perryman said.

"Is this the little deviant?" Mrs. Pesterman said throwing a finger in my direction. "I want him out of this school for what he's done to Kurt."

My parents didn't know what was going on, but huddled close to protect me. I was amazed that someone could lie with no problem, guilt, or worry about their evil. I also thought Mrs. Pesterman should get an academy award for best supporting bullying mother.

"What kind of parents are you," Mrs. Pesterman spit at my mom and dad, "letting your little criminal hurt my son!"

My dad was a hard man to ruffle.

He said, "Madam, we've just arrived. Perhaps we should hear from the boys what happened, and then yell at them."

"Hear from the boys!" Mrs. Pesterman spewed as if venom might leak out of her mouth. "Are you an idiot? Look at my son's face, and what was in your little rat's backpack."

As if on Mrs. Pesterman's payroll, the nurse pulled out the mace from my bag and set it on the table.

"See," Mrs. Pesterman said flinging spit from her over-heated jaws. "You want to hear what happened? Kurt get over here."

Kurt moved one step too slowly for Mother.

"Now!" she yelled.

He jumped to her side, his face purple with bruises and dried blood sticking around his mouth as if he were a sloppy Kool-aid drinker.

Kurt told his story, perfectly, through tears of pain, or fear of his mom. It was hard to tell. There are always two sides to every person. I felt sorry for this side of Kurt Pesterman. My parents listened to Kurt's home-practiced version and looked at me with a small shutter of doubt. They knew the mace was a set-up because I had explained the story that night and they knew I didn't have any idea where to get a hold of mace. The rest of the story had them a little dumbfounded. Doubt or no doubt, they still supported me.

"Perhaps, we should hear Handy's side now," my dad said, in an even and calm voice.

"His side!" screamed Mrs. Pesterman. "We can see his side in my son's face. All we need now is the police to get here." She turned to the principal. "If you don't call the police, I will have you fired. I know three school board members. You won't be able to get a job as principal of a kennel."

There was a knock at the door as if the universe didn't want the principal to lose his job.

The principal spoke, "I did call the police, madam. I think we will ALL now listen to what Mr. Greatneck has to say."

I looked at both my parents in the eyes and took a long sad look at Kurt Pesterman. Would I be him if I had lived his life?

"I'm sorry it has come to this," I said, "but I just have one thing to say." I paused for a second as I reached into my coat pocket.

"Thank you, Grandma."

***

Kurt and his mother both let out a confused groan as I pulled out my 512MB ultra sensitive shock resistant digital recorder, and placed it on the principal's desk. I pushed play.

"Just calm down, he'll show up"

The voice was very clear. The entire recording was as clear as a glass door at a window washer's house. I turned it off as Kurt began screaming from Jack's blows. The police had come late to this party and looked confused as if they were listening to an old radio drama. The nurse moved first and handed them the can of mace.

"It's good we have the police here," Principal Perryman said, "but I believe it is you, Mrs. Pesterman who will be taking a ride to the station."

The police officers signaled for Mrs. Pesterman to come with them. She was about to argue, until one of the officers reached for his handcuffs. Kurt watched his mother escorted from the room. She didn't even acknowledge him as she was leaving. Loyalty to bullies is a one way street.

"Mr. Pesterman," Principal Perryman said to Kurt after the door closed. "Your father is here, and he is waiting in the nurse's office. He will take you to a doctor. He hopes you would want to stay with him for awhile.

"My dad," Kurt said as if those two words relieved his pain.

The nurse started to lead Kurt away; he turned to me and said, "I'm sorry, Handy."

"Can we go?" my mom asked the principal.

"Yes," he replied, "but I would like it if Hannibal stayed. In the army we called it debriefing. I think there's a lot more going on in this school that I may need to know. Is that true, Mr. Greatneck?"

"A problem or two," I said.

"Okay then," my dad said, and turned to me. "Come home right after school. You're grounded."

I hoped he was kidding.

I asked the principal, after my parents left, if Ralphie and Kayla could come down and fill in the pieces I couldn't. They were around long before I took over the ball in this game.

15

The principal listened to Ralphie and Kayla's story as if it were the plot of a reality television show his parents forbid him to watch. He looked alternatively riveted and repulsed by how such things could be happening in the world and stupid because everyone knew all about it but him.

I filled in my pieces, the ones not on the tape, and we all sat quietly contemplating the school's future for 1.4 seconds before Principal Perryman jumped up and ran out of the room like he'd just realized he'd left a faucet running somewhere back in 1985.

We sat and looked puzzled at each other until Ralphie broke the silence. "How long do you think it will take him to get to the border?"

I don't know if the thought of Principal Perryman driving like a bank robber toward Mexico to avoid dealing with this recent revelation was the funniest thing I'd ever heard, or if the 6,000 pound monster truck of a realization driving off my chest, that this case was over, caused my reaction, but I started to laugh. More accurately, I fell over myself with hysterics, and like a quickly spreading virus I infected Kayla, who began to giggle in spite of the fact that she wasn't sure she even understood what Ralphie was talking about.

Ralphie joined in by smiling with one side of his mouth and slowly nodding his head up and down. For most people this would be considered an acknowledgment of humor, but for Ralphie it was major guffaw action.

Principal Perryman was gasping for air as rushed back into the office.

"What's so funny?" he asked.

I wiped the tears off my cheeks with the back of my hand and tried to remember what exactly had been so funny.

"Nothing, sir," I said. "I think we're a little relieved."

"I can see that, Mr. Greatneck," Principal Perryman answered back, trying to catch his breath and a little uncomfortable that we might be laughing at him.

"I went to get the teachers," he said, "but they've all gone home."

"It's 6:15 p.m.," I said pointing to the large white clock on the wall that seemed to lord over every elementary school room as the harbinger of good or evil depending on when you looked at it.

"Yes, it is very late," Principal Perryman said as if he'd just come out of a seven-year coma and couldn't believe his beanie babies were worthless. "I guess tomorrow we can tell the teachers about what has happened."

We all headed to the door with the same excited feeling a person gets when they've finished running their first marathon. Exhaustion was kept at bay by the adrenaline of accomplishment, but man, I would be sore in the morning.

"Oh, Mr. Greatneck," the principal stopped us as we moved into the outer office, "I did see the janitor, and he says you owe him a new key chain." A silent understanding passed between us as I had left the janitor's part out of my story. Principal Perryman left it at that and we headed out of the front door of the school startled by the night sky. We walked Kayla home without speaking, talked out by the principal and knowing we had many years as friends to talk.

Kayla spoke just before she went into her house. "The drive to the border thing wasn't that funny." With that she wrinkled up her nose in a way so cute I started to believe in Santa Claus again, and she whirled into the house.

We went home.

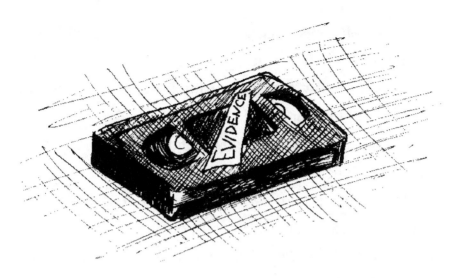

16

With no help from us, the story of what happened whirled around the school like a cyclone, but this time Dorothy's house came down on Zach Brewer and Jack Greenblatt. As is the case with most bullies, they turned on each other and Kurt like starving weasels when confronted with the tape. My tape was police evidence, but was also played for the PTA, teachers, and the school board along with our stories. The truth about William B. Travis had truly set us free. The cage disappeared like a sour smell in the refrigerator that you finally found and pitched into the garbage.

"Do you think we'll see Kurt again?" Kayla asked about a week later as we slurped our slushies on the picnic table near Mr. Fresh that was only half covered with bird droppings.

"I don't know," I said. "I think his dad is going to home school him for a while."

"I feel sorry for him," Kayla said as if she thought we might smack her as a traitor.

"Me too," I said. We both looked at Ralphie who slowly raised an eyebrow before speaking.

"What? I'm an ogre?" he remarked, taking a long slow draw off his slushie straw. "I feel sorry for the people who don't think I feel sorry for Kurt Pesterman."

That was enough for us.

"Hey, Handy, what's our next case?" Ralphie asked.

"Yeah," threw in Kayla, "and I want more to do on the next one. Like going undercover."

"Let's just see what comes up," I said. "Something always comes up."

Appendix
Not Feeding the Bully

Everybody is bullied in his or her life. As you get older, the bullies change their tactics, but it is no less stressful. Maturity and education is a great source of power against bullies. To lessen any type of bullying situation takes four steps that are easy to remember.

1. Stay calm.
2. Assess the likelihood of violence.
3. Have a thick skin and a sense of humor.
4. Collect evidence.

1. Stay Calm: When I was cornered in the locker room, I was scared and emotional, but it is important to hold it back. No matter how much fear I felt, I was not going to show it. Bullies eat fear and grow bolder from it. I also was not going to get angry. Retaliation and threats are only a way to destroy your life a hundred times worse than you were bullied. Your goal is to take the fun out of the situation for the bully by staying calm and quiet.

Do not play their game.

2. Assess the likelihood of violence: Most bullying is threats, insults with the intent on degrading you, and physical intimidation. If I thought I were in danger of getting physically hurt, I would have gotten away as fast as possible and reported the incident to the school, my parents, and the police.

You want to be a bad target for bullies, not a punching bag or store. If you are assaulted, or worse, things are being stolen from you, these are crimes and must be reported. The problem is most bullying ends up being their word against yours, and teachers and parents have little power to stop what no one has seen. Even when they know it's going on, the authority around you has little power to act without evidence of trouble, and many times the bully's parents will be loudest protesters of their little bully being punished for his or her awful behavior. In the locker room, I assessed quickly the Slytherin boys were not planning a fight, but that does not give much comfort when the menace is still close at hand.

3. Have a thick skin and a sense of humor: I have been called worse things than "Goofyneck." This on the insult scale lands right above "Poopyhead" on its effect on my self-esteem. Most bullies stick with targets and keep bullying them because empty words get a huge response. At my last school, a kid in my class named Ricky Brennan was even smaller than I, and had a face that toddlers would call cute. The other kids loved to call him "Little Baby Ricky" as in: (Add baby talk here.)

"How's Wittle Baby Wicky today, huh. Wittle baby Wicky are you gonna cry for us today. Baby Wicky."

On and on and you get the idea. Ricky would then cry and scream, "I'm not a baby, I'm not a baby," and freak out to the delight of every bully, and most bystanders, in the building. His bully bull's-eye was so large that a Bully Student Exchange Program was proposed so other school's toughs could share in the fun. I asked Ricky one day after he had been sobbing for half of recess, "Ricky, are you a baby?"

"Not you too!" Ricky said as he geared up for another wail.

"Wait, Ricky. Calm down," I said. "Relax and answer the question. Are you a baby?" Ricky sat for a second then said, "No, that's why it hurts so much."

"Ricky, are you a pickle?" I said.

"A what?"

"Answer the question. Are you a pickle?"

"No," Ricky said looking at me like I was nuts.

"So, if they called you a pickle you would run around screaming, I'm not a pickle. I'm not a pickle."

"Of course not," said Ricky. "That would be stupid."

"What's the difference?" I told him, "Pickle, baby, three-horned rhino. It's the reaction they want and you give it to them like a performing baboon." I actually had Ricky's full attention. "It's rule number one in the bully handbook. Pick something they know you are sensitive about and hammer away. We all know you have a face that makes the Rugrats look mature."

Ricky laughed which sounded more like a hiccup and punched me in the arm, "Jerkneck."

"See, now you've got a sense of humor," I said. "Use it to move their target away from you."

"Yeah, but that was funny, Handy," Ricky said. "I'm not quick with the comebacks like you."

"You don't have to be. Stop being destroyed by every slur. Silence is a great tool against bullies. When they start up, just look bored, and after a couple minutes, check your watch and say, "You guys finished? I've got class.""

"But I don't wear a watch."

I thumped Ricky on the head

"Ouch!"

"That's not the point," I said. "Pretend you have a watch. Take the fun away from them. You might even get to the point where they are uncomfortable."

"And they'll stop?" Ricky said a glimmer of hope in his eyes.

"No," I said, "but after a while it will be boring for them, and they will spend less and less time targeting you and probably end up just throwing an insult your way from time to time. More importantly, you won't care as much and it will be a lot easier."

"Thanks, Handy. You should be a psychologist."

"No, pal, I'm a detective," I said. "Jerkneck, now that hurt my feelings."

4. Collect evidence: As my new locker room buddies were throwing lame insults my way, I was looking around and remembering. Zillions of bully victims tell on their aggressors only to be seemingly ignored by teacher and parent alike. This is partly because they look like tattletales with nothing to back up the fact that they are pushed around more than the only lawn mower on a sod farm. Think of yourself as a detective. Collect evidence of the time, place, what was said, and who was involved.

Better yet, it is the twenty-first century. Get a voice recorder. Some record for hours and have 500 or more mega-bytes of space. Make sure it's small and keep it running all day if necessary. You will record everything said by the bullies. Remember that you are recording yourself! Watch what you say. You need to be heard on the same recording not being mean, abusive, or threatening retaliation. If you are throwing insults back, then you are as guilty as those around you. After collecting around ten instances of abuse, make a CD of one after the other with a written log of times and places. This is hard evidence to ignore.

Your next move is to set up a meeting with parents, teachers, you, and the bully all in the same room. The more maturely you approach this, the more you will be taken seriously. This tactic is incredibly difficult, but shows you are serious about change. The bullying may not totally stop, but you will be more respected and perhaps the teachers and staff will supervise a little closer. Present your evidence, be calm, and let your tormentor tell his side. Do not become agitated or upset by anything said. The bully or his parents may try and degrade or verbally attack you or the school. This all looks better for your case.

Also, propose solutions that make sense for stopping the bullying.

Here are a couple examples:

1. The bully and his cohorts do not talk to you and are to stay away from you at all times. In addition, you will stay away from them.

2. Ask for more supervision. Two schools ago the major portions of the bullying went on in the locker room after gym because the gym teacher wouldn't so much as stick his head in there and the bullies knew they were beyond detection. There are lazy and careless teachers. Don't be hurt by their unwillingness to protect you in the school. Get four or five students together and make a list of recommendations of places in and around the school where kids are taunted. Present it along with parents and maybe even go to a school board meeting if no action is taken. Ask why teachers cannot be more of a presence in those areas. And be persistent! It takes lots of time and effort to create positive change, and there will be many people trying to stop you. You will find some parents and teachers are as big a bullies as your peers.

One school's biggest bully was the son of a teacher in the same school. This teacher would scream and yell at anyone who would suggest her little cutie pie, a thirteen year-old the size of Arnold Schwartznegger, could ever bully anyone.

3. Get other students involved. If you can make a pact with four or five others to step up and stand with the kids being bullied, it sends a message that bullying is not cool. When a group of bullies starts picking on someone, everyone else seems to abandon them because they don't want abuse to be attracted to them. How do you feel when abandoned by them? You don't have to be friends to help each other. You don't even have to like each other, but you do have to stand together. Coming to the aid of those being bullied can make situations easier to handle for the bullied and less fun for those taunting.

Make an anti-bullying pact so if one person is being picked on by a person or group then five or more kids get up and stand with the bullied. The anti-bullying group does not retaliate, return insults, act violently, or become verbally abusive. Just stand together, be calm, non-combative, and supportive. It is a whole lot easier to have a thick skin and hold down fear when you have sympathetic company.

These are not easy solutions, but doing nothing and taking abuse with no action will eat away at your self-esteem like termites in a Lincoln Log house. There will always be bullies. It takes action and work on your part to strengthen your character and affect change. We have all been the targets of a bully. Our goal should be not just to sympathize with those now being bullied, but also to stand with them, and not become bullies ourselves.

Hannibal Greatneck III, Detective

For more information or to contact Brad about visiting your school or venue, or ordering books for schools or libraries, go to:

www.dontfeedthebully.com